Andy Opens Wide

by Nan Holcomb

illustrated by Dot Yoder

JASON AND NORDIC PUBLISHERS
EXTON, PENNSYLVANIA

Other Turtle Books

Sarah's Surprise
Patrick and Emma Lou
Cookie
A Smile From Andy
Danny and the Merry-Go-Round
Andy Finds a Turtle
How About a Hug

Library of Congress Cataloging-in-Publication Data

Holcomb, Nan, 1928-
    Andy opens wide / by Nan Holcomb ; illustrated by Dot Yoder.
        p.   cm.
    Summary: Andy, who is five and has cerebral palsy, has difficulty
opening his mouth at mealtime, until his frustration leads to a
discovery.
    ISBN 0-944727-06-9
    [1. Cerebral palsy--Fiction. 2. Physically handicapped--Fiction.]
I. Yoder, Dot, 1921-   ill. II. Title.
PZ7.H6972Ap 1990
[E]--dc20   90-4501
                                                      CIP
                                                       AC

ISBN 0-944727-06-9
Printed in the U.S.A.

For Jason,
his Mom and all other Jasons and Moms
who get discouraged.

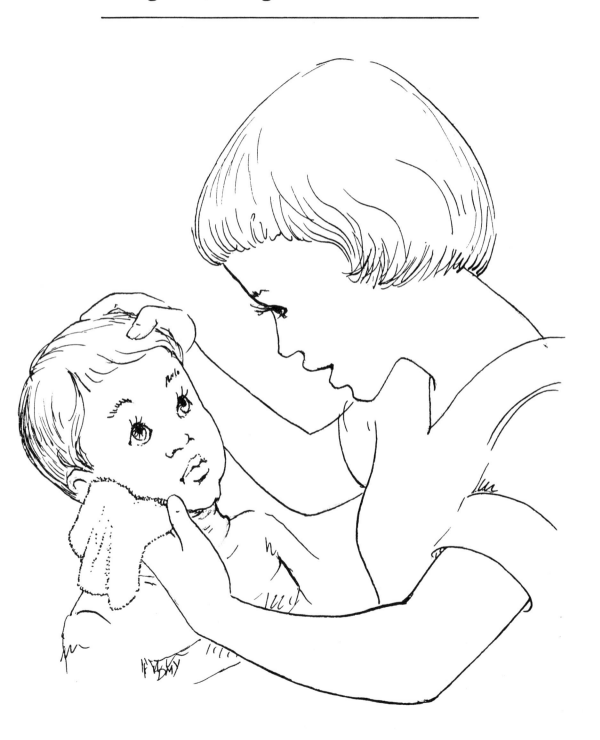

One day Andy couldn't open wide
no matter how he tried.

"I'd like to give up," Mommy said
as the oatmeal oozed and slipped and
dripped — outside — his tightly closed
lips.

Hey! Don't give up, Andy thought.
I'm hungry! So . . .

Andy tried and tried.
Mommy poked and pried.

At long last the oatmeal was all
inside. Mommy felt tired and cross.
Andy felt very discouraged.

Andy closed his eyes and tried to
hide. Then . . .

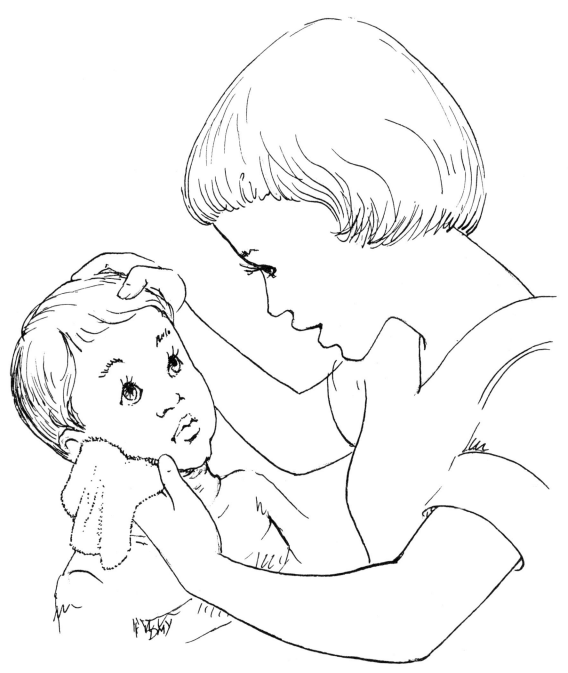

Mommy washed his face. She gave
him a kiss and said, "You just keep
watch. One day you'll learn to open
wide."

Keep watch? Andy thought.
Sounds great! But, what do I watch?

Doors that open wide?

Or jars all filled with **things** inside?

Or — is it **who?**

He watched Baby Sue. She really
did open wide! Mommy had to hang on
tight or spoon, hand and arm could
have disappeared inside!

Baby Sue knew how to open wide and she didn't know very much at all. Andy closed his eyes and tried to hide. Until . . .

he heard Buff, the cat hop down and
begin to lap his milk. Buff opened wide
and he was just a yellow cat.

Andy closed his eyes and tried to hide.

Then he heard a little bird.

There on the window ledge right outside, a little fat bird had opened wide and swallowed a seed. Even a bird could open wide.

Andy closed his eyes and tried
to hide. But then he heard . . .

"If you wake up, I'll take you for a ride!" There stood Dad in boots and jeans. "A ride," Dad said and opened wide.

Andy started to close his eyes, then
he remembered . . . he liked to ride!

Strapped in good and tight, he sat
next to Daddy, high up in the truck. off
they drove to the farm for some milk.

A calf stood by the fence, opened
wide and bawled, "Maa-a-aw."

Andy looked his meanest look at
that brown calf. He didn't close his
eyes to hide. He was getting just
plain —

MAD inside . . . even a cow could open wide!

He still felt very cross as they rode over the hill to the big feed mill.

Dad climbed down and went inside. Andy
felt much too mad to hide. He didn't
even close his eyes. Just then . . .

a big black dog ran across the yard, put his paws on the truck and opened wide. He gave Andy a kiss with his long red tongue.

The big black dog could open wide, but Andy couldn't be mad. He couldn't feel sad. So, he smiled — just a very small smile — because that day his mouth wouldn't open wide.

"Hey, fella!" Dad called. "You're coming inside."

Before Andy knew what was
happening, there he sat propped

between two bags of grain with five
fat, happy little puppies climbing all
over him. Noses in pockets, noses
down neck, they romped and played all
over those sacks. Soon . . .

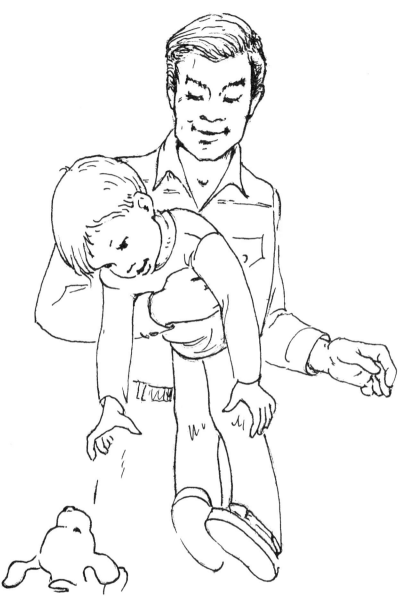

"C'mon, fella. It's time to go back,"
and Daddy just picked him up from
those sacks. Andy didn't want to go.
But, nobody asked. Dad just picked
him up like any old sack and fastened
him back in the car seat.

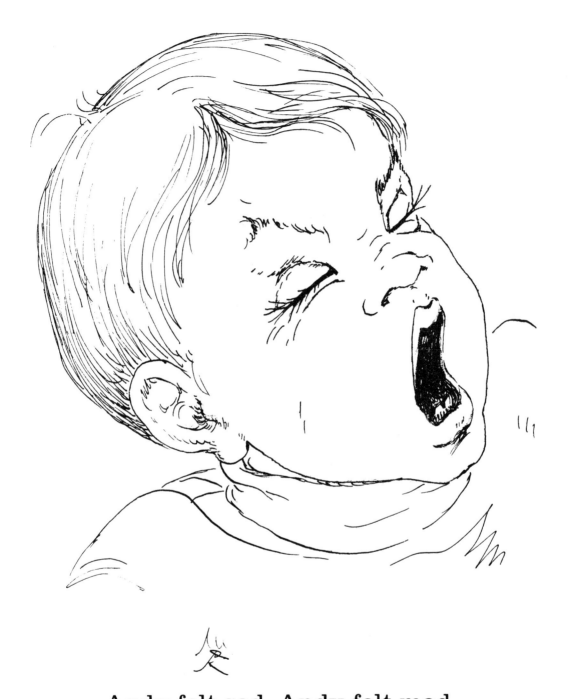

Andy felt sad. Andy felt mad.
Andy opened his mouth wide and
started to yell. He cried. He bellowed.
He howled.

Daddy just sat and waited and watched.

Then, Dad shouted, "That's the biggest, widest open mouth I've seen in years!"

Andy stopped yelling and . . .

rolled his eyes from side to side. What
a surprise! He'd opened wide! Slowly
he shut his mouth — but not too tight!
What a surprise! He **could** open
wide! He wouldn't ever again,

have to hide from Baby Sue —

or the cat —

or the bird —

or the calf.

His mouth **did** work and one day he just knew he'd learn to open wide whenever he wanted to.

So he smiled his biggest smile and enjoyed his surprise!

Then he hummed and Daddy whistled all the way home.